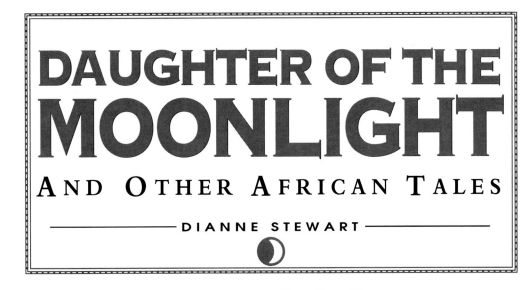

DAUGHTER OF THE
MOONLIGHT
AND OTHER AFRICAN TALES

DIANNE STEWART

ILLUSTRATIONS BY Gina Daniel

STRUIK

Contents

Introduction

Africa folktales were originally not written down, but were passed on from one generation to another by word of mouth. They were performed live and although the same folktales were told many, many times, they were never exactly the same.

Folktales introduced the audience to a world of dreams and fantastical characters. They were not only entertaining, but also a means of education, and reinforcing cultural and social standards. These enchanting tales also offered possible explanations for the mysteries people encountered in their own world.

In traditional societies in southern Africa there is a taboo against telling folktales during the day, for fear that the storyteller would grow horns. But if the daily tasks were completed and grandmother or great aunt could be persuaded to tell a story before the sun had set, both the storyteller and the audience would put a piece of wood in their hair just above their forehead to prevent horns from growing.

But folktales were also performed to a larger audience. It is said that men were expert tellers of animal tales, because they knew the wildlife so well. In these tales, the animals keep their own appearance and identity, but they behave and speak as humans do. The greedy Hyena, for example, is easily fooled. Although Elephant is slow, he is reliable and thinks things over carefully. And although Tortoise is also very slow, he is very wise and is the only animal who is able to outwit Hare, the trickster. Jackal is deceitful, selfish and greedy.

The folktales in this book come from a wide variety of sources and I have tried to be as true to the original as possible, providing some insight into the very rich oral tradition that has flourished in the fields of Africa.

Dianne Stewart

Dianne Stewart

The sun and moon of the San people

———————— San ————————

Long, long ago, when there were not as many people living on the southern tip of Africa as there are now, the San people spoke of a time when the sun was a man who lived amongst them. When the sun man lifted his arm, light streamed from his armpit and the world basked in its warmth, but when he lowered his arm again, the world became dark and cold.

One day a childless San woman spoke to another woman as she sat in the sun, her children playing happily around her.

'I have been watching the sun man and he seems to be growing old. He spends much of his time sleeping. Tell your children to gently lift up his arm when he is asleep, so that bright sunlight can shine from his armpit.'

'Yes,' added the mother of the children. 'It is cold without his light and warmth.'

Then the childless woman continued: 'Tell your children to lift the sun man onto their shoulders and throw him into the sky, so that he can truly become the sun, and warm us all the time.'

So, later the San children crept along the soft sand, leaving a trail of footprints behind them, like the spoor of an animal. They hid behind a clump of thorn bushes, and waited for the sun man to lie down and sleep.

The children watched as he knelt, then lay down, stretching his body out on the sand.

He lifted up his arm and rays of sunshine lit up the clumps of grass and spreading plants which grew around him. For a while it was bright and warm.

'Keep very still,' said the eldest child. 'Don't let him see us.'

When the sun man lowered his arm, the children shivered as the cold descended on them. But after a while, they heard the sound of his heavy breathing, carried to them by the gentle breeze as it danced playfully around them.

'He's asleep,' whispered the eldest child.

Creeping forward as quietly as hunters stalk their prey, the children approached the sun man. They checked that he was still asleep, then lifted his arm. They were bathed in bright light.

Then, working together, sharing the weight of the load, the children lifted the sun man up onto their shoulders, and they were greatly warmed by just touching him.

'Remember what the old woman told us to tell him,' said the youngest San child.

5

When the sun man became almost too hot to hold, they hurled him up towards the sky, saying:

'Man of the sun, become the sun in its fullness. Stay in the sky, so that you will light up the land and take away the darkness. As you travel the sky, give us warmth so the *San rice* will dry and we'll be warm.'

As he moved upwards with his arms outstretched, bright light shone from the glaring sky. Then he became round like the sun and was no longer a man.

When the sun was in the sky it was bright and the San people could see one another clearly. The children found grasshoppers and flying ants. The men hunted eland, ostrich, springbok and gemsbok, and the women looked for food.

When it was night, the sun disappeared over the horizon, taking away its light and then the moon appeared to lighten the darkness.

But the sun would chase the moon away again, and it was told to the San children at the time that the sun stabbed the moon with its knife, so that it slowly became smaller and smaller.

The moon protested to the sun: 'The children need just a sliver of light.' So the sun agreed to allow the backbone of the moon to remain. But when the moon shrunk until it was no more than a thin sliver, it went home in great sorrow. It couldn't give much light. But then it put on a new stomach and became whole again, like a full moon.

And the San reminded their children that Mantis so disliked the dark that he threw his shoe up into the sky and *it* became the moon. So the new moon drifted through the night sky feeling like the shoe of the Mantis.

Many moons have passed since the first time the San told this tale to their children. And as the bright moon cast its light on them, they were reminded of the time when the moon was once also a man who could talk. He took Tortoise aside and told him that he was entrusting him with a very important message to deliver to mankind.

'Tell the people that as I dying live again, so you dying will live again.'

And so Tortoise started out early as he knew how long it would take him to reach the people.

'As I dying, live again,' Tortoise repeated quietly to himself over and over again as he crossed the sand. 'As I living ...'

But the more he repeated the message to himself, the more confused Tortoise became, and it wasn't long before he had to admit to himself that he had forgotten the message completely.

There was only one thing to do. Tortoise turned around and began retracing his tracks on the return journey to the moon.

'I am very disappointed in you, Tortoise,' said the moon angrily. 'I will have to think of another plan.'

The moon, brushing Tortoise aside, called on Hare and said: 'As you are a fast runner, deliver this message to the people: As I dying, live again, so you dying will live again.'

Hare skidded off across the sand, running as fast as he could. But he soon came across the tender, young shoots of a green plant, and was distracted. He stopped, caught his breath and began to nibble on them hungrily.

Suddenly he remembered the moon's message: 'As I live, dying ... as I dying live ... which was it?'

Hare panicked. He had forgotten the moon's words, but he was too scared to go back to moon to find out what it was.

And so he ran on towards the people, playing with words in his mind, arranging and rearranging them until he was convinced that he had remembered the correct message.

Then the Hare said to the people: 'The moon says: "As I dying live again, so you dying will die forever."'

When the moon heard that Hare had delivered the message incorrectly, he was so angry that he split Hare's lip with a stick. That is why, say the San, the Hare has a cleft upper lip.

Mantis and the storytellers

Some African people explain the origin of the sun and the moon through ancient tales passed down from one generation to the next. The San are known to be Africa's great storytellers. But many San stories also tell us about animals who had, in a time almost forgotten, once been people. Perhaps the most respected of these extraordinary creatures was the praying mantis. In San mythology, the Moon is represented as the shoe of the Mantis, which he threw into the sky to give him light. Mantis had as his wife Dassie or Rock Rabbit. Some of these creatures may still be seen in the remarkable rock paintings left behind by the San people.

San or Bushmen rice is a term for termite or ant eggs which are considered a delicacy.

The hungry jackal

Khoikhoi

A wind appeared from nowhere and set the landscape in motion. Gusts swirled above the earth, gathering up the dry red dust which caked the sparsely scattered bushes and tufts of bristly grass.

It carried the scent of Black-backed Jackal to the sheltered place where Spotted Hyena lay sleeping under a bush. By the time Hyena had come to her senses, Jackal had slinked closer and closer, carrying his tail upwards over his back.

'On the prowl again, Jackal?' asked Hyena, with a hint of curiosity in her voice.

'I'm always on the lookout for a good meal,' laughed Jackal, scanning the horizon as he spoke.

White clouds built up in the distance and the wind chased them across the usually empty sky. Then a low bank of cloud blew towards Jackal and Hyena, and seemed to hover above them in the lower reaches of the sky.

'There's fat,' said the scavenger Jackal, dashing towards the cloud as it stretched out before him. He leaped onto the mountain of cloud and was carried across the sky by the wind.

Hyena was amazed and fixed her gaze on the clouds as the wind pinned her round ears back and ruffled her tawny grey mane. All she could see was Jackal's bushy tail peering through a gap in the grey-tinged cloud.

Suddenly, Jackal's satisfied face, with its long pointed ears and sharp snout, appeared over the edge of the cloud. Jackal shouted to his friend: 'Hyena, I've eaten all I can. I want to get off this cloud. I'm a long way from the ground. Please catch me when I jump down.'

Hyena said nothing.

'Please, Hyena. I'll share my wonderful feast with you,' pleaded Jackal. 'There is more than enough fat up here for you too.'

'Jump then, Jackal. I'll catch you,' laughed Hyena.

So Jackal fell down towards the dusty earth and Hyena caught him, breaking his fall. When he had caught his breath, Jackal said: 'Right, Hyena, it's your turn now. Wait for a low cloud to pass and then run and jump up onto it.'

When the clouds came nearer, Hyena ran towards the horizon and jumped onto a bank of cloud. It rose up, up, up into the windswept sky and carried Hyena along with it.

When she had eaten as much as she could, she leant over the edge of the cloud and called down to her tawny friend: 'Jackal! J-a-ck-a-l! I want to come down. Please break my fall.'

Cunning Jackal replied: 'Look, my friend, my hands are out-stretched, ready to catch you.'

Down, down fell Hyena. But just as she was about to fall into Jackal's arms, he screamed:

'Wait, Hyena! Wait! I've been pricked by a thorn. Ouch! Ouch!'

'Too late! I can't wait,' cried Hyena, plunging with lightning speed towards the ground.

Spotted Hyena landed with a thud. She was hurt by the fall and lay crumpled on the ground. And since that day her left hind foot has been smaller and shorter than the right foot.

In days gone by, this is the story the Khoikhoi, or Hottentots, told their young children to explain why Hyena seems lame in her back legs when she first starts to walk. But they also had many, many other tales about wily Jackal that told of both his cunning and crafty ways.

They tell, too, of how the sly Jackal tricked the foolish Hyena out of a magnificent feast. The story, as told by the Khoikhoi, is something like this:

The wooden wagon was packed with glistening, gleaming fish that had been caught earlier in the day. A helper signalled to the driver of the wagon and together they began to haul their heavy load across the white sands that lined the blue-green waters of the Cape.

The afternoon sea-breeze carried the salty tang of the waves with them as they climbed the steep slope that flattened out at the top of the cliff.

The scent of fresh fish caught the attention of Jackal as the wagon trundled slowly along the bumpy old road that led away from the coast. Led by his nose, he kept his distance at first, slinking along behind the wagon, unnoticed by the two men on the wagon seat.

Jackal tried to think of ways of getting into the wagon from behind. But it seemed impossible to do so without being noticed. Then cunning Jackal had an idea. He ran along the side of the road, hidden by the bushes that grew along the track, until he was well ahead of the wagon.

Then he lay down in the middle of the road and waited. He grew restless when he couldn't hear the wheels of the wagon as they gouged their path along the road.

'Perhaps the wagon has stopped for the night,' Jackal thought. 'Or perhaps the drivers have decided to take another route.'

But, after a while, Jackal heard the creaking wagon in the distance and he lay very still. When the wagon was almost upon him, the helper shouted to the driver: 'Look at that jackal lying there dead in the middle of the road. You could turn him into a fine kaross for your wife.'

'Good idea' answered the driver, but as he was eager to continue on his journey, his helper casually flung the jackal onto the back of the wagon.

As the light faded and Jackal bumped along in the back, he threw fish out onto the road, one by one – leaving a trail of shiny silver fish behind the wagon.

When he had thrown out enough fish for a feast, Jackal leapt off the back of the wagon and hungrily gobbled up the fish. He tore at the fresh flesh, and licked his lips.

Jackal was so busy savouring every mouthful that he hadn't noticed Hyena slink up behind him. Hyena, too, was hungry and began to help herself to the fish that lay strewn across the road.

Jackal watched angrily as he saw his supply of fish quickly disappear into Hyena's stomach.

'Why don't you do as I did, Hyena?' said Jackal peering at his friend. 'Lie very still on the road in the path of the wagon and you'll also be thrown onto the back as I was.'

Hyena took the advice and waited at the side of the road for another wagon to come by. Eventually she heard the groaning and creaking of wagon-wheels and lay down in the road ahead of the wagon.

When he was almost upon the animal, the driver said: 'What an ugly beast! Get out of the way!'

Taking a stick, he prodded Hyena, who was too scared to do anything but remain as still as if she were dead. And instead of being thrown onto the back of the wagon, like Jackal had said, the wagon continued on its journey without her.

Hyena picked up her bruised, sore body and hobbled off to find Jackal. Jackal had already eaten his share of the fish and had given the rest to his family.

'Poor Hyena, you missed out on the fish,' said Jackal, pretending to feel sorry for his friend.

'Perhaps we should have swopped skins!'

Men of Men

The Khoikhoi, or 'Men of Men' as they call themselves, lived in the Cape of Good Hope long before the Dutch arrived and settled in the area in 1652. They were given the name Hottentots by the European settlers. Although they are similar in many ways to the San people, the Khoikhoi were herders of cattle, sheep and goats while the San were traditionally hunters and plant-gatherers. It is thought that the Strandlopers, who once lived along the coast around Table Bay (now Cape Town) and who ate mostly shellfish and plants, might also have been part Khoikhoi.

The milk bird

Xhosa

It was spring and the villagers came to life as though they were waking from a long winter sleep. From sunrise to sunset, the Xhosa people worked in the fields, preparing the dry ground for seeds. As they loosened the iron hard earth with hoes, they dreamed of the first spring rains that would soften the ground and bring life to their planting.

Khethani had been dreaming of the rain that never came for many seasons now. The drought-stricken village in which he lived had had just enough grain to see them through the winter. Still, Khethani was hopeful and worked long hours in his fields.

One night, while the people slept, a bird perched on top of a tree near Khethani's field and said:

'Weeds, grow again in Khethani's field.'

The weeds obeyed the bird and when Khethani and his wife arrived at their field the next morning, they were surprised to find their land unweeded.

'That's strange,' said Khethani, 'the land we dug up yesterday is covered over with weeds again.'

'We must start again,' said his wife, picking up her hoe. The sun warmed their backs and by the time they returned home with the other villagers at sunset, Khethani and his wife were stiff and tired, but satisfied that their work had been done.

That night the bird returned and gave the same order: 'Weeds, grow again in Khethani's field.'

The next morning, when Khethani and his wife saw that their land was covered with weeds again, they cried out to their neighbours in despair.

'Perhaps this has happened because you are lazy,' the other villagers laughed.

Once again, Khethani and his wife started uprooting the weeds and worked until sunset. When the smoke from the first fires danced above the rooftops in the village, Khethani said to his wife:

'I am going to hide near our field tonight and see who or what is destroying all our hard work. You wait for me at home.'

As he lay in wait, Khethani saw a bird hover above a tree and then land on one of its silhouetted branches. It was such a beautiful bird that he fixed his gaze on it. The bird flew down and hopped along the ground, and Khethani was utterly amazed when he heard the bird say: 'Weeds, grow again in Khethani's field.'

Khethani was so angry that he ran at the bird and was about to grab it, when the bird cried out: 'Khethani, don't harm me. If you spare my life, I'll make milk for you.'

'First you need to restore our fields,' said Khethani angrily. 'You have given us extra work.

The bird fluttered its wings and said: 'Fields of Khethani, become weeded again.' And Khethani watched as the weeds became uprooted and then ordered the bird to make milk for him. He took out a calabash and the bird filled it with thick warm milk.

Khethani savoured the milk as it slithered down his dry throat. It had been a very long time since he had tasted milk.

Khethani hid the bird in his bag, and when he arrived home he said to his wife: 'Wash all the largest pots we have.'

'What for? You are teasing me!' said his wife. 'You know that we are experiencing famine and are hungry. What food do you intend to store in the pots?'

'Just follow my instructions and you will soon see,' said Khethani.

When the pots were clean, Khethani gathered his sleepy children around the pots and told them to watch. He took out the bird and said:

'Bird, Bird make sour milk for my thirsty family.'

The children watched in awe as the beautiful bird made sour milk for them, filling all the pots.

'Just remember, children,' said Khethani, 'tell no-one about this bird. Not even your best friends.'

The next day, happily fed, Khethani and his wife continued to cultivate their fields. It would soon be time to plant maize, beans and pumpkins.

One day, when the children of the village were playing near Khethani's house, little Nomsa said: 'Children of Khethani, why is it that you are fat and we are so thin?'

Khethani's children looked at each other and said: 'But we are no fatter than you are.'

But the children of the village did not believe them and kept nagging and nagging Khethani's children to tell them their secret. Eventually, Khethani's young daughter whispered: 'There is a special bird in our father's house that makes thick milk for us.'

'Can we see it?' the children asked in disbelief.

Checking that their parents were still working in the fields, Khethani's children led their inquisitive friends into the quiet house.

'Where is it?' asked one of the children, looking around curiously.

Khethani's daughter took the beautiful bird from the secret place where it was hidden and asked it to make milk for all the children. Obediently, the bird did as it was asked and, after drinking the sour milk, the children said: 'Let the bird free for a little while so that it can fly around and stretch its wings. It is such a beautiful bird!'

Suddenly, the bird flew out of the house and, stretching its wings, soared high into the cloudy sky.

'Our father will be very angry,' cried Khethani's eldest child. 'We must follow the bird. Quickly!'

All day long the children chased the bird, not even stopping when they had a stitch in their side. When the bird rested on the ground, they tried to grab it, but it took off again, landing in trees – always out of the children's reach.

As the sun neared the hills in the west, the villagers left their fields and returned to their homes. Khethani looked at the grey clouds and said to his wife: 'We are sure to have rain tonight. Look at those mountains of cloud. But where are the children? They normally run to greet us.'

They searched the house and yard frantically and when Khethani saw that the bird was missing too, he knew what must have happened.

The setting sun was darkened by heavy clouds and the light disappeared quickly. The village children were a long way from home and feared a storm.

'Let us forget about the bird and return to our parents. Listen to the thunder roaring in the distance.'

'Do not be afraid,' said one of the older boys, 'I will look after you all.'

So the boy made a shelter for all the children and they gathered wild roots, and toasted them on a fire. As they were eating, a cruel old man mysteriously appeared from the shadows and demanded their food. They were terrified.

'Give him the roots,' said the elder boy, and while the man gobbled up the food, the children escaped, running as fast as a buck. But when they turned around, they saw that he was following them...

'Let's hide in that forest,' said the boy, leading them to a dark forest at the foot of a mountain.

'You'll be safe here,' he assured them. 'Climb that tree and stay there.' So the children sat shivering in the dark, clutching the branches of the tree.

After a while, the children saw a bird with the largest wing-span they had ever seen. It appeared out of the darkness and hovered over them.

'Cling to me,' said the eagle, 'I will take you home.'

Flying through the darkness of the cool night, the bird took the first children home. Then he returned again and again, trailing the sky with his *kewee-kewee* until all the children were safely home.

Khethani and the other parents were so relieved.

'Where have you been?' they asked.

'We thought you would be angry when the bird escaped so we chased it,' cried the eldest child.

'I am so relieved you are safe,' said their mother.

The milk bird never returned, but Khethani, ever hopeful, said: 'We are sure to have rain soon so that our crops will grow and flourish.'

And as he said this, the first drops of rain hit the dry, iron-hard earth.

Milk of Africa

Amasi, or maas, is a thick, naturally soured milk, rather like yoghurt, enjoyed by many southern African people. This curdled milk, like most dairy products, is not only very nourishing and healthy but is also quite cheap and forms the basis of many traditional tribal dishes. Amasi may be mixed with vegetables, and is also used to make cottage cheese. Because it is so popular and is part of the staple diet of many people, amasi can now also be bought in shops.

Frog's first croak

Zulu

Dawn brought the first gentle light to the scraggy, drought-ravaged thornveld. Slowly, the sun began its climb into the orange-tinged sky and gathered its strength for the long journey to the west.

Animals began to emerge from the silent shadows. Warthog and her young crept out of the aardvark hole where they had sheltered for the night. Noisily they scrunched their way through the dry undergrowth, heading towards the water. They were not the first to arrive at the shallow waterhole. A herd of graceful, tan and white impala who were quietly drinking fled in fright as Warthog staked her solitary claim to the muddy shallows of the drinking place. Frog watched her from a log at the edge of the murky water. She and her young rolled and snorted with delight as the mud caked their hairy bodies.

'She really does take over the waterhole,' grumbled Frog to himself.

But not for long. Soon Warthog was joined by zebra, giraffe and a herd of nyala. When she discovered she was not alone, Warthog left the muddy water and scratched her itchy back against a tree. Her young waited impatiently nearby. Suddenly there was a hush amongst the animals at the water's edge. They had heard a cry, and listened keenly as the cry came closer and closer.

'Its the side-striped jackal himself,' said one of the zebra. 'I wonder what he is doing up so early?'

At the sight of the trickster the animals around the waterhole became uneasy.

Jackal spoke immediately. 'There seems to be very little honey about,' he said.

'Yes,' agreed Nyala bull, tossing his head back. 'I've noticed.' Nyala was especially fond of honey. In fact, all the animals had noticed that honey was scarce. They all liked it very much, and suddenly everybody had something to say about the shortage.

'I say,' said Jackal screaming to make his voice heard above the drone of discussion, 'that whoever finds honey should be allowed to eat it.'

'Agreed,' said Nyala bull. 'As long as the animal who finds it can get past the bees who are guarding the honey. When bees have honey, they're as vicious as a wild dog with a bone. I've been stung many, many times!'

'That is always a problem,' laughed Zebra, lifting her head from the foal she was gently grooming. 'I think all the honey that is found should be shared amongst us all. After all, we are all partial to the fruit of the bees.' The animals agreed.

'I have an idea,' said Giraffe, straightening his legs after taking a long drink of cool water. 'I have been listening to the discussion and I think it would be a good idea to take the matter to Elephant. He is the largest and wisest of us all and he'll be able to help us decide how we are going to share the small amount of honey that is left in the thornveld.'

'Yes,' said Nyala. 'Elephant's many years in the bush have given him great experience and wisdom.'

'Why not leave the matter to me? I'll decide who will have the honey and who won't,' offered the wily, side-striped jackal. But no-one trusted Jackal.

By the time the animals had set off to find Elephant, the sun was almost a quarter of the way on its journey through the sky. It shone down brightly, warming the already dry and dusty earth.

Old Elephant bull, who lived alone, was wallowing in the slow flowing waters of the river when the deputation arrived. He seemed to ignore them as they waited for him on the river bank. He squirted himself slowly with cool, brown water as the animals continued to squabble amongst themselves on the bank above him. After a long wait, Black Rhino stood apart from the animals and put himself in charge of the deputation.

'Elephant, we need you to settle an argument that has broken out over the shortage of honey this year.'

Elephant flapped his ears. Then he spoke.

'I know,' he said. Elephant knew everything.

'I've been listening to the arguing and I think the best way to settle the dispute is to declare that, because there is so little honey, none of the small animals should be allowed to eat any honey at all.'

'Not a bad idea,' said Black Rhino. 'After all, they do have very small appetites, unlike us larger animals!'

Grey Duiker, Mongoose, Suni, spotted Hyena and even muddy Warthog were not at all pleased with the new ruling.

'We have been discriminated against because of our size,' said Suni.

Frog had arrived just in time to hear the judgment and he too was very unhappy with the ruling. The small animals murmured and grumbled amongst themselves, but were too afraid to speak out against Elephant's decree. But Frog, who had been stunned into silence, could simply not keep quiet any longer. He enjoyed fresh, dripping honey as much as any other animal and never before had he been told that he could not eat honey.

'Why should only the *LARGE* animals be allowed to eat honey? That is terribly unfair!' Frog spoke in a deep melodious voice and surprised even himself that he had been so outspoken.

'Frog is right,' chorused the small animals. His boldness had given them courage.

'Silence!' thundered Elephant, flapping his huge ears in anger. 'Who dares challenge my ruling?'

Tortoise, suddenly endowed with enormous courage, stuck out his neck and begged Elephant for the chance to say something.

'Kind Elephant,' said Tortoise. 'Don't you think that it would be fairer if none of the animals ate any honey for a whole year? Maybe then the bees would have made enough for us all to enjoy.'

The animals couldn't believe that Tortoise had dared to make a suggestion to Elephant.

A debate followed, interrupted only by the sound of Lion's yawn in the distance. A hush fell over the animals. Frog, knowing that he had the support of the smaller animals, and angry because he was denied his rights because of his size, burst out:

'Excuse me, Elephant, but I cannot live without honey for such a long time ... and there are many animals here who would agree with me ...'

'Please be quiet, Frog,' whispered Suni. 'You're spoiling it for the rest of us.'

Then, in a loud voice, Elephant replied. 'I need time to reconsider the matter.' He realized that his wisdom should be just and fair for all.

So the animals waited restlessly on the river bank, while Elephant pondered the matter of the honey.

Finally Elephant said: 'We have an agreement. No-one may eat honey for a whole year. Anyone found breaking the law will be punished.'

By the time the agreement was reached, the sun had already moved on, leaving a trail of scorching heat which sent the animals clambering back into the thornveld in search of shade.

The hot days crept by and poor Frog began to regret that he had spoken out so boldly. More than anyone else in the thornveld, Frog craved honey. And when the honeyguide fluttered his wings and flew around in circles, drawing attention to a hive, Frog found it very hard to ignore him. The bird's distinctive chattering cry was a great temptation to a honey-lover. One day, when Frog was out searching for food, he saw a swarm of bees foraging for pollen and nectar. Making sure that no-one was around, Frog traced the path of the bees back to their hive in the hollow of a dead tree, not far from the reeds where he lived.

While planning a way to get at the honey without being stung, he suddenly remembered Elephant's warning. Reluctantly, Frog turned back. He resisted the temptation to steal the honey and tried to forget all about the sweet, drippy substance he so loved.

But one day early in Spring, he noticed a huge swarm of bees leaving the hollow tree.

'They're looking for a new hive,' he thought.

So, late that afternoon, as the setting sun cast its finger-like shadows on the thornveld, Frog went out to find a little taste of honey. The sun was disappearing quickly, taking most of the light with it.

'No-one would mind if I had a taste,' he reassured himself. 'In fact, no-one would even see me,' he thought. Frog looked around in all directions. There was no-one around. He checked again and then hopped towards the tree.

He was pleased to see that there were fewer bees guarding the honey than before. In the tree were glistening pieces of honeycomb, dripping with dark golden honey. His mouth watered. He leaped forward towards the comb with great courage. His heart pounded in his chest. He helped himself to a mouthful of honey.

'Delicious!' he said, as the sweetness clung to the inside of his mouth even after he had swallowed it.

When Frog had finished, he looked longingly at the comb again, wishing that he could have a little more. But he decided against it. He couldn't take the chance. He was already feeling a little guilty.

As he leapt home, still savouring the taste of honey in his mouth, Frog heard a voice in one of the trees above him. He hopped more quickly, trying to hide in the wheat-coloured grass. He heard the voice again. It seemed to be following him. He froze. Frog was beginning to feel very frightened indeed. His eyes stuck out even more than usual. Someone must have seen him! Frog felt so guilty about what he had done, he could barely speak.

'I'm s..o..rr..y' he croaked. 'I'm so s...o...rr...y,' he replied to the voice above him, in a deep voice that sounded like a bellowing, young calf.

Frog was so choked up that he had great difficulty forming the sounds of the words in his throat. Not only had he eaten the honey, but someone had seen him do it! He had also betrayed the trust of all the animals in the thornveld.

He never did discover who the voice belonged to, but Frog had learnt his lesson. From that day on, Frog's eyes always looked as if they were about to pop out of his head. And, even today, Bullfrog always croaks in a loud, booming voice – and never, never eats honey!

The Flight of the Honeybee

A bee colony can consist of 60 000 bees – all busily contributing to the tiny community within a hive. There are three types of bee in the hive and each has special duties. The queen bee is the mother of the colony and lays the eggs. She is cared for by the infertile females, called workers, who feed the larvae and clean and protect the hive. When a hive is disturbed, the workers will protect it fiercely, and an angry swarm can be quite dangerous. Male bees are called drones, but only one drone mates with the queen.

The cattle herder's song

Swazi

In a fertile valley, west of the Lebombo Mountains, lived a king who had a large herd of fine cattle. In fact, it was one of the largest herds in Swaziland. The king valued his beasts so highly that only his son was allowed to take care of them.

Early every morning, the boy would take his father's cattle out to graze. At night, he would call each by name and herd them home to the kraal.

On dreamy summer days, the boy would open the kraal gate and drive the cattle to the river. They were led by a magnificent ox with fine horns and a loud voice, so when he bellowed all the cattle followed.

The boy would sit on the rocks at the edge of the river and watch the weavers build their nests and the swallows swoop down to drink. Sometimes he would sit in the cool shadows of the rocks where moss and little ferns grew.

But as much as he loved his father's cattle, the king's son often grew tired and longed to sleep, especially at midday when the sun's heat is greatest. But he forced himself to stay awake so he could watch the animals as they grazed in the long grass.

One summer day as he lay on a rock, with the heat waves rising up around him, the boy fell asleep and thought he was dreaming. A gnarled, old woman stood beside him. He sat up in fright.

'Don't be afraid,' said the woman. 'I'm here to help.'

'It is such a responsibility to look after my father's animals,' the boy said. 'They are so important to him that if one cow strays or is stolen, I'll be in great trouble. I have to wake early in the morning, and I often get so tired out here in the heat of the sun.'

The old woman smiled: 'Look at that large round rock worn smooth by the river.'

The boy looked at the rock and was sure he had never seen it before.

The woman continued: 'It is so wet and slippery that anyone who tries to climb it will fall into the river. But you shall not fall. That will be your rock. Stand on it and you will be able to see the whole river valley. You'll be able to follow the course of the river as it slithers around the bends like a snake, and you'll see *all* your father's cattle in one glance.'

The boy was so excited that he ran towards the large smooth rock.

'Wait, son,' the old woman warned. 'Never fall asleep on that rock or your cattle will be stolen. I will teach you a special song, and when the cattle hear it, they will all come to you and follow you wherever you wish to lead them.'

The boy listened as the wind whipped up the grass around him and the river flowed by lapping at its edges. Then the old woman sang her simple song:

Cattle, cattle far away,
Come to me and do not stray.

The boy practised it and when he had mastered the tune, he saw his animals ambling towards him from all directions. He turned around to thank the old woman for her kindness. But she had gone.

All through the summer the boy sang to the cattle and they never strayed or were stolen.

One day the air in the valley was so hot and humid that the king's son lay down on his special rock to rest. It was a quiet day, with no wind to rustle the sweet-reed on the other side of the river bank and cool his face. He fell asleep.

The people on the hillsides noticed that the herder was asleep and slowly crept down into the river valley. They gathered all the cattle together and drove them away, led by the magnificent ox.

When the king's son awoke, refreshed by his sleep, he stood up on his rock, stretched and looked for his cattle. They were gone. In desperation, he sang his special song as loudly as he could.

Cattle, cattle far away,
Come to me and do not stray.

But there was no response, not even an echo.

Panic-stricken, he ran up and down the river bank, thinking that the cattle might have strayed, but by nightfall he had still not found them. He dreaded going home.

When he arrived home and told his father that his cattle had gone, the king was so angry that he said, 'Go and search for my prized possessions! You are not welcome here until you return with my cattle.'

The boy wandered down to his stone at the river's edge. With the dim light of the half moon, he climbed up onto the slippery rock, and cried.

Suddenly, he felt a hand on his shoulder.

'I told you not to sleep,' said the old woman. 'Now your cattle have been stolen. But, go to the chief who has your cattle and ask him to take you on as his herder.'

At first light, the young boy walked along the mountain paths, through many cultivated fields and at last he reached the settlement of the chief. He heard the bellowing of the ox and knew immediately that his father's cattle were in the chief's kraal.

He begged the chief to let him watch the cattle. The chief agreed, so the boy worked for many years, thinking of a way to return his father's cattle.

In the mornings when he took the animals out to graze and in the evenings when he returned home with them, the boy sang his special song. Although he longed to be with his own family, he was comforted by the fact that he was with his father's cattle.

One year, at the time of the First Fruits Festival, the king's son saw that beer had been prepared by the women and had been placed in a row of calabashes outside the kraal. All the men, women and children had gone to the fields with their baskets to gather the first ripe produce of the harvest: maize, millet, ground-nuts, sugar cane, and pumpkins.

Only the king's son and an old woman who was too old to do any work were left at home. The boy had a plan. He ground a special herb into a fine powder and put a little of it into each calabash. This would make the drinker sleep.

The celebrations began, and the first fruits of the harvest were brought to the chief. His advisors gave him and all present a purification drink of sea water and river water, mixed with herbs. Then, while the king's son watched from afar, they ate the first fruit ... and drank the beer.

Not one was awake to see the full moon rising, except for the cattle herder who had not taken part in the celebrations. He crept off to the cattle kraal and, opening the gate, sang:

Cattle, cattle far away,
Come to me and do not stray.

The boy led his cattle past the sleeping villagers. The sound of their snoring drowned the clomp of the cattle's hooves and no-one stirred. By the light of the full moon, the king's son escaped with his father's cattle. Clumsily they made their way across the countryside. At sunrise, the ox in front bellowed so loudly that all the cattle from the east, west and south, came to join them.

With a sense of urgency, the boy drove the cattle towards his father's kraal, only allowing them to graze or drink at the river for a short time. But when the chief woke to find his cattle missing, he called his warriors together and, with their shields and assegais, they followed the tracks of the cattle.

Towards evening, the king's son heard the chief's men in the distance behind him. He drove the cattle down from the hills into a thickly wooded area that lined a stream.

The boy hid beneath a fig tree. He was very scared and didn't want to lose his cattle again. Darkness fell. He was cold and lonely. He knew that he had to think of a plan before dawn. At first light, the chief's men would start following him again.

The mosquitoes irritated him, the frogs around him croaked so loudly that he couldn't sleep and bats scuffled in the branches above him. Suddenly, he heard a voice. It was a voice he recognised.

'Do not be afraid,' said the old woman. 'Just do as I tell you. Kill one of your white oxen and make ten thousand little shields out of the hide. I will bring you warriors of your own.'

The boy looked at the woman in disbelief, but he did exactly as he was told. Then the old woman turned to the frogs and said:

'Each one of you must take up a shield and be a warrior for the king's son.'

All through the night the boy instructed them, and just before the darkness of the night gave way to the gentle rays of the morning sun, the boy ordered his army of frogs to sit in a row on the hillside, so that the chief's men would clearly see the warriors and their shields.

When the chief and his men saw the great army of frogs and heard their war-cries, they were terrified and retreated into the valleys. Although the chief was desperate to retrieve his cattle, he decided that he would rather lose the cattle than his men.

So, after the cattle had grazed on the sweet grass, the king's son sang his song and continued his journey to his village. The cattle followed contentedly.

The king was overjoyed to see his son. He hugged him and gave him great honour.

'You have looked after my cattle well, son,' he said proudly. 'And they have increased in number.'

And so, every morning and every evening, the king's son sang his special song and the cattle neither strayed nor were stolen.

The Festival of the First Fruits

The annual First Fruits festival is still celebrated in Swaziland today in gratitude for the harvest. The celebration starts three weeks before the summer solstice with a ceremony called the 'little incwala'. A group of men go off to the west to collect river water, while another group journeys to the east to find sea water. On their return, the king and his attendants withdraw into a secluded hut called the inhlambelo, where the king tastes the first fruits of the season and the traditional sweet-reed. When the dancing and singing begins, the people know that they can eat the harvest. The 'big incwala' takes place at full moon less than two weeks later and lasts for six days. There is dancing and sacred songs are sung. The young men of the village cut branches from the sekwane thorntree to reinforce the king's hut and a black bull is killed. The ceremony then ends with a huge bonfire in which the remains of the slaughtered bull, a section of the crops and items used by the king in his inhlambelo, are burnt.

Hen and Hawk's lost friendship

—— Sotho ——

Long ago in the mountain kingdom of Lesotho, a special friendship developed between Hawk, a bird of the air, and Hen, a bird of the earth. Hawk loved to visit Hen. Whenever he came down to earth to talk to Hen, she would stop whatever she was doing, flap her little rust-red wings and cackle and cackle as she listened to Hawk. They were very good friends.

Now, Hawk had a treasured possession that no other bird in the kingdom owned. It was a shiny, silver needle and he kept it carefully hidden in his home high up on the mountain ridge. Hen knew about this needle and one day when Hawk was visiting her, she asked:

'Dear Hawk, please may I borrow your needle?'

'Whatever do you want to do with my needle?' asked Hawk in astonishment.

'I'd like to sew a new blanket for myself. The summer is nearly over and it gets so cold when the snow covers the mountains.'

'Dear Hen,' said Hawk. 'You know it is the only needle amongst all the birds, what will happen if you lose it?'

'I promise I won't, Hawk,' pleaded Hen. 'I'll only use it myself and take very special care of it. If I lose your precious needle, you can have something precious of mine.'

'And what is that?' Hawk asked.

Hen paused for a moment and thought about what was dearest to her in all the kingdom. And, knowing that she would certainly guard Hawk's needle with her life, offered him one of her most treasured possessions.

'A chick,' Hen answered confidently. 'One of my precious, little children.'

'Fine,' agreed Hawk. 'That is a fair exchange. Your young chicks must surely be as special to you as my needle is to me, so I know you will look after it well.'

Hawk took off into the clear blue sky with his strong wings and Hen watched until he was but a little black dot in the distance. Then she gathered together her little skins and laid them out – ready to start patching them together to make her blanket.

She was so happy to think that she would soon have a *Hlosi*, a magnificent skin blanket fit for a chief or one of his wives.

When she looked up into the sky again, Hen saw Hawk already making his way back to her from his mountain-top home. In his strong, hooked beak he carried his gleaming needle. With a promise to take good care of it, Hen took the needle and Hawk flew off in search of breakfast. Hen threaded the needle with a long thread and using fine stitches, she carefully sewed her skin blanket. When it was finally finished, she wrapped it around her and showed it to her family.

'You look more beautiful than any other hen on earth,' said her family. This pleased Hen and made her feel very proud. She walked up and down, showing off her new blanket. She felt like a very special person, as grand as the wife of a chief in her new *Hlosi*, and was so flattered when fowls that she didn't even know came up to her and said: 'Hen, you look very beautiful. Just like the chief's wife.'

When all the hens in the village had seen her blanket, Hen quickly called together all her chicks and said:

'I do not want my new blanket to get dirty. Please clean the house for me. Gather the dirt together and put it all on the fire heap so that it is ready to be burnt.'

Then Hen went strutting off to show her new blanket to the hens who were working in the fields. So proud was she. She even forgot all about Hawk's needle.

Hen's little chickens cleaned her straw house from top to bottom, swept the floor and threw all the dust onto the fire heap as they had been told to do. 'Mother will be pleased with us,' they chirped. 'There is not a speck of dust anywhere.'

But Hawk's precious needle was hidden amongst the dirt ...

The hens weeding the fields admired Hen in her new blanket. 'You look so radiant, Hen; as beautiful as one of the chief's wives.'

All the compliments had gone to Hen's head and she strutted home proudly, forgetting the words of her forefathers who said: Pride comes before a fall.

Suddenly, as Hen was following the little path through the grass that led to her home, she saw a large dark shadow on the ground in front of her. She recognised her dear friend, Hawk, but she had forgotten all about his needle and the promise she had made to him.

Swooping down to the ground, Hawk said: 'Hen, do you realize how proud you have become in that smart blanket of yours?'

She giggled and, taking no notice of him, kept on walking along the path. Then Hawk said to his friend: 'I have come for my needle, so I can put it back in its very special place.'

Hen jumped. She got such a fright. She suddenly remembered the promise she had made to Hawk and the price she would have to pay if she lost his precious needle. She didn't say a word but hurried back to her little house.

When she arrived home, she saw that the floor was spotlessly clean. There was not even a speck of dirt on the floor. There was no needle either. She looked everywhere for it.

'It must be on the fire heap,' she said, running outside. She ran as fast as she could to the edge of the village, where the fire heap was still smouldering. Hawk hovered above Hen, watching her as she searched through the fire heap, desperate to find the missing needle.

Hen could see the worry in Hawk's penetrating eyes and she scratched and scratched, frantically looking for the lost treasure. She didn't even notice that her blanket had fallen off her back and it lay in the ashes on the fire heap.

Hawk flew off to give her a little time, but when he swooped down again from the sky, Hen knew he had come to take her chick. She moaned and groaned in anguish. She ran to protect her children, tucking them safely under her wing. But Hawk was not an unreasonable friend, and he flew off again so that Hen could scratch around in the dirt a little longer. When he had disappeared the chicks went back to scratching for food.

Hen clucked and cackled and was a little relieved, but she was still worried. Not long ago she had felt like the wife of a chief, but now she was nothing. She didn't even know where her new *Hlosi* was, and she felt like a mother who could not even protect her own young.

'I have to find Hawk's needle. I must find it.' she cried out aloud.

The hens in the village were worried about her. She looked so distressed. Hen told them what had happened and they felt very, very sorry for her. They were mothers too, and understood how she felt. So they helped her look for Hawk's needle. They looked in the long grass, they looked along the dirt paths. They even looked through the fire heap again. No-one could find the needle.

Then, as Hawk flew over them, he cast his sprawling dark shadow across the paths of the hens and they shrieked in terror. They were very frightened. There was no guarantee that Hawk would not take one of their children.

'Chicks, come quickly and hide under our wings,' they cried to their children.

They never found the needle. No, never. It was lost forever. Hawk was so disappointed and angry that he never again visited Hen. Their friendship had been lost and was replaced by fear and distrust. Fear and distrust.

The Sotho Blanket

Because winters in Lesotho, the traditional home of the Sotho people, is so cold and snow covers the mountains, the Sotho blanket has become the national costume of its people and is still worn by many Sotho today, particularly those living in rural communities in and around Lesotho. The colours and designs of these blankets change with fashion, and may even vary between different age groups. A Sotho man traditionally wears his blanket pinned across his right shoulder, while a Sotho woman wears her's pinned across her breast. These brilliantly coloured and beautifully patterned blankets may be decorated with a wide variety of different symbols and designs.

The hunters and the honeyguide

— Zulu —

At the first sign of morning, Jabane and his elder brother, Mandla, set out for a day of hunting. Mist, like soft smoke, swirled in the valley below, hiding the stream that lay like a sluggish snake in its sandy bed.

'I'm after an impala today,' said Mandla excitedly.

'I'd be happy with just a bushbuck,' said Jabane, adjusting the strap of the shoulder bag he carried.

As they tramped their way through the scratchy, long grass and dry, spiky bushes, the mist lifted and the sun shone brightly in the clear sky.

'There's a clearing over there between the trees,' said Jabane. 'Let's walk towards it.'

When they reached the open space, they came across a very strange sight indeed. Large brown-red coiled pots had been placed upside down in a straight line on the grass.

'What are these pots doing out here in the middle of the bush?' asked Mandla, astounded by what he saw before him. Jabane was fascinated and leaned over to touch them.

'Leave them alone, Jabane,' warned Mandla nervously. 'There's something strange about these pots.'

'I want to see what is under them,' answered Jabane, handling the first one. 'See, Mandla! There's nothing under it!'

Mandla crept a little closer and watched cautiously as Jabane picked up the second pot. All that was under it was the imprint that the mouth of the pot had made on the grass. Confidently, Jabane picked up the next pot and the next, as though playing a game, until he came to the last pot in the row.

'What are you afraid of, Mandla?' laughed Jabane.

But as he turned the last pot in the row, an old woman stood up and stretched.

Jabane screamed and stepped backwards, distancing himself from the pots.

The woman was stooped with age, and her smiling face bore the lines of one who had spent many, many years wandering the veld, looking for food.

She walked right past Jabane and said to Mandla:

'Stop shaking liked a scared, young buck. I won't do you any harm. Come with me. I have something wonderful to show you.'

But Mandla would have nothing to do with this woman and he ran away. Then the old woman turned to Jabane.

'Come with me, young man,' she said to him, urging Jabane to follow her.

Jabane followed the old woman as she hacked a path through the dense, spiky veld with an axe. The midday sun scorched their skin and Jabane grew hot and tired. He was relieved when the old woman eventually stopped in front of a Sweet Thorn tree.

'Young man, take this axe and cut down this tree,' said the old woman.

Jabane looked up at the size of the tree. It was huge and it would take him hours, even days to cut it down. But he was too frightened to disobey her.

He lifted the axe, gathered his strength and struck the tree as hard as he could. With the first strike, a copper coloured ox appeared out of the tree. Jabane couldn't believe what he had seen.

'Strike again,' urged the woman, smiling.

So he struck the Sweet Thorn again and a tan coloured cow came out of the tree trunk. With each strike a bull, cow, goat or sheep emerged, until Jabane was surrounded by animals.

'Take these animals home, young boy,' said the old woman. 'They are yours. I will remain here.'

Jabane was shocked.

'Thank you,' he said gratefully, looking at all the livestock. Then he drew the animals together and started herding them back home towards his father's village. When he passed the clearing, he found his brother, Mandla, asleep against the trunk of a tree.

'Awu, Jabane! Where did all these animals come from?' asked Mandla, jumping up.

'Walk with me, and I will explain,' said Jabane.

As they drove the animals homeward, Jabane told his elder brother what had happened, arousing great jealousy in Mandla's heart. The journey through the bushy veld was slow and after a while, Mandla said: 'I need water. Let's leave the animals to graze and see if there's a stream or spring nearby.'

They climbed over a rocky outcrop and were on the edge of a steep and treacherous cliff when Mandla shouted to Jabane: 'There's a trickle down there. Let me down with a rope. I'm parched.'

Jabane skilfully made a rope out of creepers and lowered his brother down from the rocky outcrop high above the little stream. When Mandla had quenched his thirst, Jabane hoisted him back up and said: 'My turn now.'

Mandla let Jabane down, down, down to the rocks beside the stream. While Jabane was drinking and washing his face in the water, an evil thought came to Mandla. He threw the edge of the creeper rope over the cliff and smiled to himself as he ran back to the animals. Mandla knew that his brother could never climb out of the ravine on his own.

He found himself a strong stick, and Mandla drove the animals home, away from the setting sun. Jabane and Mandla's father ran out to greet him when he appeared on the outskirts of the village. 'Mandla! Where did you get all those animals?'

Mandla told them about the old woman.

'But where is Jabane?' asked the boy's mother.

'He took another route home,' lied Mandla. 'Isn't he home yet?'

'We've not seen him,' said the boy's mother. 'And it will soon be dark.'

'He can take good care of himself,' said his father. 'Perhaps he's still out hunting.'

Darkness fell and covered the village. Then, when it lifted the next morning, the women set out to draw water from the sluggish stream in the valley. A surprise greeted them at the water and they returned in a hurry to their husbands: 'We've heard the honey-bird calling in a tree near the stream. Quick, follow it and fetch some honey for us.'

The boys' father and some village men ran after the honeyguide, keeping their eyes on the bird's white tail feathers as it made pathways through the sky.

The bird led them into thick bush. Some men were tired and said: 'There's no honey. We're going home!' But, at that point, the honeyguide flap-flapped its wings mightily and screeched its call '*whit-purr, whit-purr ... whit-purr ...*' urging the men to follow.

As the bird hovered above a rocky outcrop, Jabane's father stood still and listened.

'I hear a faint cry from the ravine below,' he said. 'Listen ... it sounds like my son.'

'J-a-b-a-n-e!' he shouted.

The honeyguide flapped its wings and then took off, swooping down into the rocky ravine below, landing next to Jabane.

Jabane's father looked over the rocky edge and saw his son. He quickly made a rope out of creepers, let it down and hoisted Jabane up to safety.

'If it weren't for the honeyguide, we might have lost you,' sighed Jabane's father, putting his arm around his son.

As they walked home, Jabane told his father what had happened. 'Your brother will be punished,' he said. 'His jealousy has made him act foolishly.'

But, by the time the villagers arrived home, Mandla had disappeared. He had heard that his lost brother had been found, and he knew that Jabane would tell his story.

Jabane took care of his cattle, sheep and goats. Not only did he prosper, but he remembered his parents in their old age and took good care of them.

The Honeyguide

The little honeyguide is found mostly in Africa, and features quite commonly in popular African myths and folktales. Some species are known to lead men or animals, such as the familiar honey-badger or 'ratel', to the hives of wild bees by making chattering noises, and flying in the direction of the bees' nests. Once the hive has been raided, the honeyguide eats what is left. It feeds on bees' wax and grubs, and the honeyguide has a tough skin and a special membrane over its eyes so that they are protected against being stung by the angry bees. Although it is more common in Africa's woodlands and thornveld, the honeyguide may also be seen in our own gardens and parks.

The test of fire

—————— Sotho ——————

Tortoise crept along a sandy, bald patch of grass, heading for the shade. Occasionally she paused, reflecting on how far she had travelled. And, of course, every now and then, she was side-tracked by the new leaves on shrubs, made succulent by the first summer rains.

Zebra and wildebeest congregated in the spiky acacia shadows, trying to escape the searing heat of the midday sun. Even the warthog retreated from the oppressive heat that hovered in the air.

Energized by the shade of the trees, Tortoise crept further and further into the undergrowth, only noticing Duiker when he stood up from his leafy bed.

'Sorry to have startled you, Duiker,' said Tortoise politely. 'It's so cool here.'

'I prefer to stay here all day,' said Duiker. 'I dare not be seen during the day. Crowned eagle has a nestling to feed.'

'So, you're not very brave, Duiker,' teased Tortoise.

'Well, you're not very fast, are you, Tortoise?' teased Duiker in return.

'Slow, but sure,' laughed Tortoise.

'Excuse me,' interrupted the warthog. 'There is only one way to test courage ... and that's by fire.'

'He's right,' said Tortoise flippantly. 'Let us put our courage to the test, Duiker.'

Duiker hesitated, knowing he was terrified of flames, but then he realised how cowardly he would seem to the other animals of the veld. So he agreed, but only half-heartedly.

The challenge attracted a great deal of interest and the grassland inhabitants crowded around.

'I'll dig a hole in which we can build the fire,' volunteered the warthog. 'And I'll also ask the springhares and moles to help me. We're all expert excavators.'

'We'll collect the firewood,' said a guinea-fowl.

'And we'll help too,' said the leader of the turtle doves from his perch overhanging the gathering.

While all the activity continued around him, Duiker took very little interest. He went back to his cool place in the wooded area and lay down lazily in the shade. Tortoise nibbled at a few juicy leaves for a while and then rested too.

It was only when the bundle of thorny firewood was placed beside the hole that Tortoise realised that the test of her courage was soon to take place.

'Duiker,' pleaded Tortoise, 'please let me go first.'

Duiker was relieved and readily agreed.

'I'm going to get some sleep now,' said Tortoise. 'I'll see you in the morning.'

Tortoise crept home and waited for night to hide the colours and shapes of the grassland. But a white moon rose in the sky, the colour of ash, and gave her just enough light to scuffle unseen through the bushy undergrowth.

She quickly dug a burrow that led out of the hole the animals had made for the fire, and then hid the entrance to the tunnel with branches. Then she went home to sleep.

The next morning, Duiker and the grassland birds and beasts had already gathered at the hole by the time Tortoise arrived.

'Thought your courage had failed you,' laughed Duiker. 'You never were very brave.'

Watched by all the animals, Tortoise went down, down into the hole and then shouted in a muffled voice: 'You can start the fire now!'

Duiker threw the firewood gathered by the birds into the dark hole and trampled it down with his hooves. Then in an elated mood, he rubbed fire-stones together causing the first spark.

The wood in the pit hissed and sparked as it surrendered to the fire. The grassland animals and birds stepped back to avoid the smoke and heat of the soaring flames.

'Poor Tortoise,' they sighed.

But, long before the flames could reach her, Tortoise had cunningly crept into the burrow she had prepared the night before. She had brought two seed-pods with her and when they were heated by the flames, they exploded in the fire.

'Tortoise's eyes have popped!' wailed the warthog.

'She should never have volunteered to go first,' said the guinea-fowl.

Duiker enthusiastically fed the hungry fire all day. It gobbled the dry sticks and branches and by dusk it had burned itself out.

Duiker went home, curled up on his soft leafy bed and fell asleep.

Tortoise slept well too. Early the next morning, she crept back along the tunnel of the firepit. After testing that the ashes were cool, Tortoise rolled around in the remains of the fire until her shell was completely covered with the ashen dust. Then she lay on her back with her eyes closed.

Duiker rose early and looked for a wild olive branch. He tore off a stick and sharpened it until it had a fine point.

'I'll never have to listen to that Tortoise again,' he said, peering into the pit.

He struck Tortoise's shell harshly.

But Tortoise slowly rolled over and answered: 'Duiker, I warned you that my courage could stand the test of fire.'

Duiker was stunned into silence. The birds and the beasts couldn't believe that Tortoise had survived the awful heat of the fire.

'Now it's your turn, Duiker,' said the warthog.

'I'm not afraid,' replied Duiker. 'How good of you all to come and witness my victory.'

Suddenly Tortoise said: 'Please would you help me dig a new hole? Duiker should have a larger and more comfortable hole than I had.'

The warthog led the work party once again and they dug all through the day.

The next morning, before the dew had evaporated in the glow of the sun, Duiker went down into the deep, deep hole. Alas! No tunnel had been built.

The firewood was put in position in the pit. It was lit and soon tongues of flames licked the air. A popping sound was heard.

'Duiker's eyes,' said the warthog sadly.

Tortoise kept the fire smouldering all day and went home at sunset.

The next day, when the acacias and wild olive trees came to life with the chorus of grassland birds, Tortoise went to the hole.

Duiker's horns were the only parts which had not been burnt by the scalding flames, so Tortoise cleaned them, shone them and made them into musical instruments. From that day on, Tortoise's song sounded through the grasslands as the wind whisked them into motion:

Poor Duiker, Poor Duiker,
He died so young,
as the flames engulfed him.
How sad!

The Blue Duiker

The timid blue duiker is the smallest antelope in southern Africa, and prefers to stay hidden among thick bush or leafy forests. It ventures out mostly at night and is usually found alone. The blue duiker feeds on leaves and fruit – particularly its favourite wild figs. Its main predators are eagles, pythons and, of course, man. Both males and females have horns and their grey-brown coat enables them to be well-camouflaged in their bushy surroundings.

Daughter of the moonlight

Xhosa

'Look at all these weeds,' sighed the young woman as her hoe hit the earth with a thud, uprooting a stubborn patch of weeds. Her husband had lost interest in her because she had not yet had a child and she carried the sadness with her as she worked in her garden.

Suddenly, a beautiful green and yellow finch landed near her and offered her some berries, saying: 'Eat these before you eat your food and you shall have the child you so long for.'

The young woman was so happy that she offered the bird her bead necklace. But all the bird wanted was river sand, which she carefully collected for him.

In time she gave birth to a beautiful daughter, whom she named Tangalimlibo, which means 'the single shoot of a pumpkin'. But the mother wanted to keep her child a secret so she hid her baby, and when the little girl was old enough to work in the fields, she would do so only by the light of the moon, and stay hidden in her mother's hut by day.

One night her father and his hunting party passed by the river. He saw this beautiful girl and watched her as she returned home with the water she had drawn. He ran after her and followed her into the hut of his wife.

'Why did you not tell me about our beautiful daughter?' he asked his wife. 'I would like to arrange a feast so that we may celebrate Tanga's growth into a woman.'

The day of the celebration arrived, but Tanga would not leave her hut until the moon rose in the sky. From the time he saw her in the moonlight, Mpunzi, the son of Jebe, wanted her to be his wife.

But Jebe said: 'Mpunzi, how can you be married to a woman who refuses to go out during the day? How will she get her work done?'

When his mother saw how disappointed Mpunzi was, she offered to help with the work and so the parents agreed to the marriage. Cattle were paid to Jebe and, as was their tradition, Tanga's father sent a cow with Tanga when she moved to the home of her mother-in-law.

Everyone was pleased when Tanga gave birth to a son. But although she worked hard, Jebe continued to try to persuade her to go out into the sunlight. And one day, when Mpunzi was away on a hunting trip, Jebe ordered Tanga to fetch water for him.

'I'll go tonight,' she said. 'When the sun has set behind the western hills.'

'Go at once, Tanga!' he said sternly.

Obediently, Tanga handed her baby to her helper, Nono, and sobbing bitterly, she made her way to the river in the blinding light of the sun. She sat on the river bank and leant over the water with her ladle. As she was drawing water, she felt the ladle slip from her hands and fall deep down into the muddy depths of the river.

'I'll try the water-jar,' she said aloud, reaching out over the water. As soon as the jar went into the water, it also slipped form her hands and fell down,

down, down. She then used the corner of her cloak, but that also fell down down into the murky water – and this time she fell down with it.

Jebe waited and waited for his daughter-in-law, Tanga, to return with his water. He sent Nono to look for her, but all she could see were Tanga's footprints in the wet mud beside the water.

'Oh! I have been selfish and self-willed,' Jebe cried. 'Look what I've done!' He looked sadly at Tanga's baby who cried and cried. Nothing could soothe him.

'I know what I'll do,' Jebe said. 'I'll drive the cow that Tanga brought with her to the river, slaughter it and offer it to the river in exchange for Tanga.'

So he went down to the water, and as he did this he cried: 'Take this rather than our beautiful Tanga.'

Nothing happened. The river flowed on as before. But then he thought he heard a whisper: 'Tell my parents that the river has taken me.'

Jebe was very worried. He could never confess to Tanga's parents what had happened. That night Jebe fell into a troubled sleep. The baby would not settle without his mother, so Nono took the child out so that he would not disturb everyone. She walked by the river singing:

Daughter of the moonlight,
Your child cries all night.

Suddenly the waters of the river seemed to part and Tanga came to take her child. She comforted him until the first light of dawn appeared on the horizon. But Tanga warned Nono:

'Never tell anyone the secret. Say that the child has grown strong and healthy by eating berries.'

So Nono crept quietly back to the hut with the child strapped to her back.

For three nights the same thing happened, until it was time for Mpunzi to return from his hunting trip. He returned home happy, laden with fresh meat for his family. He was very angry when he heard the news of his wife, but was relieved to see his son looking healthy and strong.

'What has this boy been eating?' he asked Nono.

'Berries,' said Nono hesitantly.

'Go and get some,' said Mpunzi.

But when the child was given the fruit to eat, he refused to take it and Nono was forced to tell Mpunzi the puzzling truth. That night Mpunzi and his friends went to the river by moonlight. He tied a rope around his waist and hid near the river, while his friends took the other end of the rope and hid behind some rocks.

Nono walked up and down the river bank with the baby and sang her song:

Daughter of the moonlight,
Your child cries all night.

As usual, Tanga appeared and took the child from her loyal helper. Mpunzi leapt up and grabbed them both. His friends pulled on the rope and tried to haul them up the bank, but the river rose up and flowed over its banks. The men were afraid of a flood so they dropped the rope and fled. Then the high waters of the river went down and Tanga disappeared once again.

When Mpunzi returned home, his father, Jebe, confessed that he had not sent the message to Tanga's parents. So Mpunzi asked his ox to take the message, but he would not move. He asked his dog, but the dog just barked. Only the cock would agree to take the message.

When Tanga's father received the news, he drove a fat ox back to Tanga's new home, with the cock perched on its back all the way home.

Again that night they offered a sacrifice on the bank of the river. Nono walked up and down with the child, singing the song.

When Tanga appeared, her parents took her by the hand, led her out of the water and gave her to Mpunzi. The river rose a little, then subsided and then flowed as smoothly as before.

Jebe learnt a great deal from his experience and was content to accept the fact that his daughter-in-law would never be anyone other than a daughter of the moonlight.

The Wedding Gift

The traditional Xhosa bride left her own family and lived with her husband's mother and father after her marriage. She was expected to work hard and obey certain rules in the home of her new parents-in-law. After some time, her husband built a home of his own with the help of the other men and women in the community. At the time of her marriage, the bride's father gave her a cow which she took with her to her new home and its was her's to keep. When the original cow became too old to be of any use, one of its calves took its place.

The two sisters of the Maluti Mountains

——— Sotho ———

Chief Bulane, his wife and two treasured daughters lived in the foothills of the Maluti Mountains. Everywhere they went, people marvelled at the girls' astonishing beauty and they were considered the most beautiful throughout the mountain kingdom.

Chief Bulane was also very proud of his magnificent cattle which grew fat on millet and increased in number every year.

One day, the elder daughter said: 'I would like to taste some millet.'

'No,' said her father. 'It is the cows' food.'

'You know that we don't eat millet,' said the girls' mother. 'On no occasion should you eat it.'

But the next morning when they were left alone, the headstrong elder daughter ground some of the millet kernels on a stone and then boiled them in a pot over the fire.

Hunger gnawed at her tummy and before the millet porridge was even cooked, she took some for herself and gave some to her sister to taste. 'It's so delicious,' she said, sampling the porridge.

Suddenly the girls noticed that the millet porridge was boiling over. It bubbled and bubbled – right out of the pot and onto the floor, and they could do nothing to stop it.

The younger daughter scolded her sister, saying: 'Now you know why our parents did not want us to cook this millet. They will be very angry with us when they return.'

The elder sister was terrified.

'I will run away,' she said. Hastily, she threw her blanket around her around her shoulders and fled. As she ran, the rocky ridges of the Maluti Mountains rose up to a brilliant blue sky which was untouched by a single cloud. She ran across the dusty footpaths in the heat of the searing sun as fast as a guinea fowl, not daring to look back. Her heart beat as fast as the streams that flow after the snow has melted on the mountain tops.

Suddenly, a dark shadow loomed across the path in front of her. She was so afraid that she fell to the ground, covering herself with her blanket.

Then she saw that it was Black Eagle, the mighty and powerful bird whom the mountain people called Mothemelle. Although his feathers were as black as a moonless night, the young girl remembered that he was known to be kind and gentle. She cried out:

Bird of the mountains, please rescue me.
Our parents told us not to cook millet
as it is cattle feed, but we did not listen.
Help me, Mothemelle.

And so the great black eagle swooped down, clasped the young girl firmly in his strong talons and lifted her up, up, up as he climbed the valley that led towards the very top of the mountains. There he placed her gently on the soft grass in a quiet and lonely place where there were no people. Then the great bird flew away.

The girl was heartbroken at being stranded in a strange place, but when she looked up she noticed smoke rising gently in the distance. She ran towards it and, on the other side of a small clump of trees she found a group of men cooking meat over a fire. She tried to hide behind a tree but one of the men, Masilo, got up and shouted: 'There is the most beautiful girl that I have ever seen. Catch her quickly before she disappears!'

But his companions just stared at him in amazement. Although he could certainly hear, Masilo had, up until that very moment, never spoken a word in his life.

After giving her food, Masilo took Bulane's daughter to meet his father who was a chief. Masilo's father was so pleased to hear his son speak that he gave permission for their marriage.

Masilo and his beautiful wife lived happily in their village and had two children. After the birth of their second child, Masilo's wife asked her father-in-law if she may visit her family.

They journeyed for many days until at last they could see Chief Bulane's village in the distance. The girl, drssed in her fine new skin blanket and beads, ran to greet her parents. She was relieved to find that her parents had forgiven her and they received her with kindness and great joy.

'See what Masilo's father has given you as a bride-price, Father,' she said, presenting her father with forty head of cattle.

'And these are the gifts we have brought for you,' said Masilo as he offered his mother-in-law a fine long blanket made from jackal skins, and clay pots and sleeping mats.

The daughter's homecoming brought great rejoicing. Sheep were slaughtered and there was great celebration amongst the people. Then it was time for Chief Bulane's daughter to return to the home of her husband.

Her parents were sad that their beloved daughter lived so far away, but there was one person who was very pleased indeed. Chief Bulane's younger daughter. Jealousy boiled inside her like the millet that boiled and boiled and wouldn't stop. She had heard about the beautiful black eagle that had led her sister to a handsome husband, and she wanted the same for herself.

In her anger she ran away and took the well-worn path along the foothills that join the Maluti Mountains before they rise up to reach the sky. As she was running with the dust swirling at her feet, she saw a large shadow ahead of her on the path. She looked up and, recognising the great bird, she cried out as her sister had done:

'Bird of the mountains, please rescue me.
Our parents told us not to cook millet
as it is cattle feed, but we did not listen.
Help me, Mothemelle.'

But Black Eagle scolded her.

'Younger daughter of Bulane, it is not millet that has caused you anxiety, it is jealousy. It never stops boiling inside you. You cannot escape it. It is with you wherever you go.'

With outstretched arms, she begged and begged the mountain bird to take her with him.

Then the bird, who had been hovering above her, shutting out the sun, swooped down and snatched her up, taking her into the blue heights above the rugged mountains.

Excitement grew inside the girl as they soared high above the valley. Below were her father's cattle like grains of sand on the dusty scrubland. She couldn't wait to reach the place where her sister lived.

Suddenly the black eagle dropped to the ground, released the grip of his sharp talons and left her in a quiet, lonely place not far from a little lake.

The girl could hear Mothemelle in the distance and screamed out to the black eagle: 'Mothemelle, Mothemelle, take me home.'

But the eagle was on his way home to his nest on a rocky ridge in the Maluti Mountains and he ignored her desperate cries for help.

Distraught and afraid, the young girl ran along the river that flowed from the little lake, searching for a place where she could cross it. After three long days, she found a tree trunk that bridged the water and crossed to the other side.

As she walked through the long grass on the water's edge, she thought to herself: 'That big black bird of the mountains has brought me trouble. I'll have him killed.'

But then she came across the village of her mother's brother and his wife. They welcomed her, and her vengeful thoughts were lost for a while.

'This girl's father should have found her a husband,' said her uncle. 'Now we shall have to find a man for this beautiful young girl.'

When her uncle found her a husband, Chief Bulane's younger daughter would not look at him.

'He's so ugly,' she shouted. 'My sister's husband is very handsome.'

And the next man was too old. 'My sister's husband is young,' snapped the young girl. No man seemed good enough. Eventually her uncle said angrily to her: 'You think that no man is fit to be your husband, away with you!'

And so the young girl fled her uncle's village and in her distress she cried out to Black Eagle: 'Mothemelle, Mothemelle, take me home, take me home.'

But the black eagle of the mountains did not come. So she walked for many, many days until she reached her home, exhausted.

Chief Bulane welcomed his daughter and gave her food and fine clothes to wear. 'There is a man who wishes to marry you,' he told his daughter.

'Will he give you forty cows?' she asked.

'Yes,' said her father.

'And fine clothes and beads for me?'

'Yes,' said Chief Bulane.

'And a jackal skin blanket?'

'Yes,' said her father.

'Then I will marry him,' said the young girl. 'But Mothemelle, the great black bird of the mountains has caused me great pain. He must be killed. Only then will I marry.'

So Mothemelle, the great black bird with the kind heart, was killed, and when jealousy brewed again in the young girl's heart, like bubbling millet, the bird was not around to see it.

The Mountain Kingdom

Once known as Basutoland, Lesotho, surrounded by majestic mountains, is the traditional home of the Sotho people of southern Africa. It is one of the smallest countries in Africa, and most of Lesotho's towns, including Maseru, its capital, are situated in the lowlands to the west of the country. To the east of the lowlands, lie the often inaccessible Maluti Mountains or Highlands which cover two-thirds of Lesotho. This area rises more as it continues eastward, ending in the magnificent Drakensberg Mountains which are often snowcapped. And, perhaps because much of this beautiful land is so mountainous, many rural folk still use the tough little Basuto ponies as a means of transport.

Jackal and the trusting lion

Xhosa

'Ah, ha!' said Jackal, leaving his den on the top of a rocky outcrop. 'There's Lion. It looks as though he's out hunting. A good time for some fun and games ...' Jackal thought as he clambered down the rockface.

Quietly, Jackal slinked behind Lion, imitating the bushy-maned Lion's cat-like walk as he ambled through the long grass.

Suddenly Lion roared and caught black-backed Jackal so by surprise that he stopped dead in his tracks. Lion swung around quickly and said: 'Oh! It's *YOU* again, Jackal!'

Jackal took a few timid steps backwards. 'Food is scarce, Lion, and I have four young pups at home who are s-t-a-r-v-i-n-g!'

Lion felt sorry for Jackal and said: 'Come and hunt with me, Jackal. If we catch a small buck you can have it. But if we take a large antelope, it's mine.'

'Agreed,' yapped Jackal.

So Lion and Jackal went hunting together, Jackal trotting a few steps behind Lion.

'What's that?' asked Jackal, spotting movement in the trees ahead. 'Eland' whispered Lion, stopping to observe the buck. They could see Eland's short spiral horns through a gap in the tree's foliage as the buck tore leaves from the branches.

Lion stalked his prey, crouching low in the undergrowth, and then leapt into action. He took the eland with some ease, and then, standing proudly over his victim, turned to Jackal and said: 'Go home and tell my cubs to come and eat, Jackal. I'll continue hunting in the mean time.'

'Alright,' grumbled Jackal, slinking rather reluctantly off into the bush.

He kept glancing over his shoulder and when he saw Lion disappear over the hill, he changed direction and crept off to his own den.

'My family is starving,' wailed Jackal as he climbed the rocks. 'I'd be a fool not to tell my own hungry pups about it.'

'Children,' cried Jackal, 'I have made a wonderful kill. Come and get all the spoils I have left for you.'

Back in the bush, Jackal kept guard while his little pups took the meat home. Carefully they climbed back up to their home among the rocks. Although Lion continued to hunt that day, Jackal didn't see him again. When Jackal grew tired of waiting for him, he went home to find his pups full and satisfied.

Later that day, Lion returned home and found that his cubs had been lulled to sleep by the warm afternoon sun. As soon as he lay down in the shade beside them, they woke up.

'Children, did Jackal come and tell you to go and get the eland meat?'

'No,' said the children, 'And we are s-t-a-r-v-i-n-g!'

Lion was furious. He stood up, left his family and ran towards Jackal's den. When he crossed the little stream near Jackal's house, he could hear the young jackal cubs yelling and frolicking in their home on the top of the rocks.

He tried to climb the rock up to the den, but the jackal pups threw rocks down at him. His paws couldn't grip the smooth rock and he kept slipping.

'I'll wait in the bushes beside the stream,' thought Lion. 'Sooner or later Jackal will want a drink.'

But the sun was hot, and Lion began to doze. He did not see Jackal as he approached the stream. But Jackal saw Lion partly hidden among the reeds and immediately turned tail and ran. The swish of his feet in the long, dry grass woke Lion and he quickly leapt up and gave chase.

'Rascal!' cried Lion. 'Why didn't you tell my cubs ...'

But Jackal heard no more. Seeing a small hole under a tree, Jackal crouched down low, dived into it headfirst and was almost clear when Lion caught up with him. He grabbed the end of Jackal's strong black tail and pulled it as hard as he could.

'Don't think you're holding my tail,' wailed Jackal. 'It's a root from this tree!' Lion was holding his tail so tight and the pain was so great that Jackal had to try very hard not to yell.

'Nonsense,' said Lion. 'You can't fool me.'

'Then take a sharp stone and beat my tail with it,' urged Jackal. 'If you draw blood, it's my tail. If you don't, it's a root.'

'How clever,' thought Lion, wondering where he could find a sharp stone. 'I'll prove him wrong,' laughed Lion.

But when Lion let go of Jackal's tail, Jackal slithered further and further into the hole just as he did when he was using Aardvark's abandoned burrow.

When Lion returned with his stone and found Jackal gone, he flung it down on the ground. 'I'm not being fooled that easily,' he roared angrily.

'I'll wait for Jackal to come out of the hole.'

After many hours, Jackal grew bored lying alone in the cold, damp hole. Besides, it was almost dark and he wanted to return to his family. He crept to the entrance and peeped out with his long ears alert.

'No sign of Lion,' he thought. 'I'm safe.'

He wriggled to the surface and when he stepped out into the dusk and the sound of cicadas chirping around him, Jackal yelled loudly: 'I can see you, Lion. I know you are hiding right here.'

Lion lay still, not moving until Jackal had moved just a little closer to him. Then Lion leapt up and gave chase with great powerful strides and he was just about to catch him, when Jackal sprung up onto the rock that led up to his den.

'I'll get him,' Lion said to himself. 'I'll wait until he goes out hunting again.'

And so Lion waited, and waited, and waited. And It wasn't long before Jackal was driven out to hunt by his hungry pups. Lion watched as Jackal sneaked out of his den and climbed down the rocks. Quietly, Lion padded up behind Jackal without him knowing, and let out a loud roar. Jackal could not escape, and cringed in fear before the powerful beast.

The golden-maned Lion was just about to spring on Jackal, when Jackal said:

'Wait Lion, look at what I see over there in the shadowy light. A pair of bushbuck ...'

The thought of a buck immediately diverted Lion's attention, and he looked over at the bushbuck.

'You can help me hunt them. Just wait here, Lion, and I'll go round to the other side and chase them so that they run towards you.'

'Good idea,' said Lion, crouching down on his haunches, hidden by the long grass. 'I'm ready.'

And from his den at the top of the rocky crevice, Jackal watched as Lion lay in wait for the bushbuck.

'Another day of fun and games,' said Jackal smugly.

The Trickster

The trickster appears frequently in African folktales. He manoeuvres situations to his own advantage and is able to trick not only buck but the mighty king of the beasts, the lion, too. And yet, with all his cunning, he is never able to trick the humble tortoise, who always shows great wisdom and understanding. The role of the deceitful and greedy trickster is often played by the wily jackal, and he is traditionally treated with suspicion and distrust.